# Dear Parent:
## Your child's love of reading starts here!

Every child learns to read in a different way and at his or her own speed. Some go back and forth between reading levels and read favorite books again and again. Others read through each level in order. You can help your young reader improve and become more confident by encouraging his or her own interests and abilities. From books your child reads with you to the first books he or she reads alone, there are I Can Read Books for every stage of reading:

### SHARED READING
Basic language, word repetition, and whimsical illustrations, ideal for sharing with your emergent reader

### BEGINNING READING
Short sentences, familiar words, and simple concepts for children eager to read on their own

### READING WITH HELP
Engaging stories, longer sentences, and language play for developing readers

### READING ALONE
Complex plots, challenging vocabulary, and high-interest topics for the independent reader

### ADVANCED READING
Short paragraphs, chapters, and exciting themes for the perfect bridge to chapter books

**I Can Read Books** have introduced children to the joy of reading since 1957. Featuring award-winning authors and illustrators and a fabulous cast of beloved characters, I Can Read Books set the standard for beginning readers.

A lifetime of discovery begins with the magical words **"I Can Read!"**

*Visit www.icanread.com for information*
*on enriching your child's reading experience.*

*For Ted Enik, with much*
*appreciation*
*—J.O'C.*

*For Teri, with bushels*
*of love*
*—R.P.G.*

*For R.P.G., with ongoing*
*fresh-picked thanks!*
*—T.E.*

I Can Read Book® is a trademark of HarperCollins Publishers.

Fancy Nancy: Apples Galore! Text copyright © 2013 by Jane O'Connor Illustrations copyright © 2013 by Robin Preiss Glasser All rights reserved. Printed in the United States of America. No part of this book may be used or reproduced in any manner whatsoever without written permission except in the case of brief quotations embodied in critical articles and reviews. For information address HarperCollins Children's Books, a division of HarperCollins Publishers, 10 East 53rd Street, New York, NY 10022. www.icanread.com

Library of Congress Cataloging-in-Publication Data is available.
ISBN 978-0-06-208311-1 (trade bdg.)—ISBN 978-0-06-208310-4 (pbk.)

14 15 16 17 18  LP/WOR  10 9 8 7 6 5 4 3 2  ❖  First Edition

I Can Read!

BEGINNING 1 READING

# Fancy NANCY
## Apples Galore!

by Jane O'Connor

cover illustration by Robin Preiss Glasser

interior illustrations by Ted Enik

**HARPER**

*An Imprint of HarperCollinsPublishers*

I adore autumn.

Autumn is a fancy word for fall.

The air is so crisp.

The foliage is so colorful.

Foliage means leaves on the trees.

Ooh la la!

Today our class is going on a trip.

We are going apple picking.

"I hope we pick Gala apples.

My dad likes them best,"

I tell Lionel.

He is my trip buddy.

"A gala is a fancy party.

So Gala apples must be fancy."

Lionel does not answer.

He covers his mouth and gags.

Is he carsick?

Ms. Glass shouts, "Stop the bus!"

Then Lionel laughs and says,

"It was just a joke."

Ms. Glass reprimands Lionel.

That is fancy for scolding.

She often has to reprimand Lionel.

At last we arrive at the orchard.

An orchard is a garden of trees.

Each tree is loaded with apples.

There are apples galore.

"Everyone get a basket.

Remember, do not climb

on branches," Ms. Glass says.

"There are lots of apples

near the ground."

I pick lots of apples.

Lionel juggles apples.

He is an expert juggler.

All of a sudden he stops.

He drops the apples

and runs around in a circle.

"Ow! Ow! Bees are stinging me!"

Ms. Glass dashes over.

That means she hurries to us.

Lionel laughs and says,

"I was just joking!"

"That is not a funny joke,"

Ms. Glass tells him.

She reprimands Lionel some more.

After that, Lionel behaves himself.

We pick lots of apples—apples galore.

We pick Jonathan apples.

We pick Honeycrisp apples.

We do not find a tree with Gala apples.

"Let's look over there," Lionel says,

and he dashes off.

I don't think we should go

so far away.

But trip buddies must stay together.

So I dash after Lionel.

*Voilà.*

Here are Gala apple trees!

There is one problem.

The apples are on high branches.

A ladder is by another tree.

But Lionel will not help me get it.

He starts climbing up the tree.

"Ms. Glass told us not to,"

I remind him.

Does Lionel listen?

If you said no, you are right!

Up, up he climbs.

Lionel is way out on a branch.

There are so many apples—

Gala apples galore.

Lionel shakes the branch.

The apples do not drop.

He crawls out farther.

"Be careful!" I say.

There is a cracking sound.

Is the branch breaking?

"HELP! HELP!" Lionel yells.

"HELP! HELP!" I yell too.

Kids nearby look over and laugh.

They think it's a joke.

Ms. Glass does not hear us.

She is too far away.

"Can you jump, Lionel?" I ask.

"It's too far down!" he says.

Then I remember the ladder.

I dash over and drag it back.

It is so heavy.

I perspire a lot.

(That is fancy for sweat.)

Ms. Glass is at the tree now.

She sees that this is no joke.

Together we stand up the ladder.

Lionel climbs down to safety.

*Crack!*

The branch breaks!

Down come the apples.

Ms. Glass is very mad at Lionel.

He cannot go on the hayride.

He cannot help make applesauce.

On the ride back I say,

"Thank you for the Gala apples."

I saved some applesauce for Lionel.

He slurps it down and burps.

What a goofball.

Then we each eat a Gala apple.

They do not look fancy.

But they are very tasty.

That's a fancy word for yummy.

There are plenty left for Dad.

Gala apples galore.

# Fancy Nancy's Fancy Words

## These are the fancy words in this book:

Autumn—fall

Dash—run fast, hurry

Foliage—leaves on the trees

Gala—a fancy party and a kind of apple

Galore—plenty of something

Orchard—a garden of trees

Perspire—sweat

Reprimand—scold

Tasty—yummy